DATE DUE

First U. S. edition 1990

Library of Congress Catalog Card Number 89-43618

ISBN: 0-316-11918-0

10 9 8 7 6 5 4 3 2 1

Printed in Great Britain

ONE SNOWY NIGHT

NICK BUTTERWORTH

LITTLE, BROWN AND COMPANY
BOSTON TORONTO LONDON

I t's cold in the park in winter.
But Percy the park keeper
doesn't mind.

He puts on his warm coat and
his big scarf and wears two pairs of woolly
socks inside his boots.

Percy likes to be out in the fresh air.

In the middle of the park there is a
little hut. This is where Percy lives.

When it gets too cold to be outside,
Percy goes into his hut where it's
cosy and warm.

The animals who live in the park all know Percy's hut. Every day he shares his lunch with them.

One winter's night it was so cold it began to snow. Great big snowflakes fell past the window of Percy's hut.

'Brrr,' said Percy. 'I think I'll need an extra blanket tonight.'

He made himself some hot cocoa and got ready for bed.

Suddenly, Percy heard a tapping sound. There was somebody at the door.

'Now who can that be at this time of night?' thought Percy. He went to the door and looked out.

There on the step was a squirrel. It
looked very cold and miserable.

'I can't get to sleep, Percy,'
said the squirrel. 'My bed is full of snow.'

'Oh dear,' said Percy. 'Never mind,
I've got plenty of room for two.'

The squirrel snuggled down next
to Percy and soon began to
feel warm.

Knock! Knock! It was the door again.

'Now who can that be?'
thought Percy.

Standing outside were two shivering rabbits.

'It's f-freezing,' said one rabbit.

'We're f-frozen,' said the other.

'You poor things,' said Percy. 'Come in and warm up.'

The rabbits squeezed into the bed next to Percy and the squirrel. There wasn't much room.

'Could you face the other way?' Percy asked the squirrel. 'Your tail is tickling my nose.'

Knock! Knock!

'Oh dear,' said Percy. 'Now there's someone else at the door!'

It was a fox! He looked very cold and hungry. 'Can I come in, too?' he asked.

P ercy scratched his head and
thought for a minute.

'Well, if you promise to behave,'
he said.

'I promise,' said the fox, and he
squeezed into bed next to all the
other animals.

Bump! Oops! The squirrel fell out.

'Who did that?' said the
squirrel crossly.

Knock, knock, knock!
'Good gracious!' said Percy.
'It's the door again.'

This time Percy had quite
a surprise.

There on the step were a badger,
two ducks, a hedgehog, and a whole
family of mice! They all wanted
a bed for the night, too.

Poor old Percy. And poor old Percy's
  bed! The animals pushed and shoved
and rolled around the bed,
but there was just not enough
room for them all.

    Soon the bed covers ended up
in a big, tight ball.

Then, bump! The covers rolled right off the bed and everybody fell onto the floor.

'Oh dear,' said Percy. 'This won't do at all. My bed is just too small.'

Suddenly, one of the mice pricked up his ears.

'What's that noise?' he squeaked.

Everyone listened hard. Now they could all hear it. There was a scratching, scraping sound. It seemed to be coming from underneath them.

'There's something moving under the floor,' whispered Percy.

The animals looked frightened and the mice all started to squeak at once.

'Oh dear!'

'What can it be?'

'It might be a monster!'

'With fierce claws!'

'And sharp teeth!'

The noise grew louder and louder. Then one of the floorboards began to move.

'Look out! It's coming up through the floor!'

Suddenly, there was a loud creak.

'Help!' cried the animals and they all ran to hide.

But Percy wasn't frightened. He started to chuckle. Then he laughed out loud.

A small, dark head was sticking up through the floorboards.

'This isn't a monster,' said Percy. 'It's a mole!'

'I'm sorry to burst in like this,' said the mole. 'I knocked on the door but nobody heard me.'

Percy helped the mole up through the hole in the floor, sat him on his hot water bottle to get warm and put the floorboard back.

'It's all right, everyone,' he called. 'You can come out now.'

But nobody moved. Nobody stirred. Nobody wanted to come out.

The squirrel was tucked away in the pocket of Percy's dressing gown.
The hedgehog was in his coat.
The fox . . .
the rabbits . . .
the badger . . .
and the ducks
were all safely hidden away.

The mice had even squeezed themselves into Percy's slippers!

Everyone had found a cosy bed.
'Well I never!' said Percy.

Percy yawned and snuggled down in his own bed once again.

'That's better. Now I've got plenty of room,' he said. 'And a little to spare . . .

. . . for a mole!'